Mountain Rescue Teams

capstone classroom

BTR Zone (Bridge to Reading) is published by Capstone Classroom,
1710 Roe Crest Drive, North Mankato, Minnesota 56003
www.capstoneclassroom.com

ISBN: 978-1-62521-062-3

Editorial Credits
Jennifer Huston, editor; Eric Manske, designer; Eric Gohl, media researcher

Photo Credits
Alamy: The National Trust Photolibrary, 25; AP Photo: Kevork Djansezian, 13, Todd Wells, 7; Capstone Studio: Karon Dubke, 43 (top); Corbis: Ed Kashi, 22; Dreamstime: Jørgen Melau, 40; Newscom: Bergrettung Kaprun/European Press Agency, 32, Danita Delimont Photography/John & Lisa Merrill, 37, Danita Delimont Photography/Stuart Westmorland, 38, EPA/Tom Dubravec, cover, 10, picture-alliance/dpa/Frank Leonhardt, 35, picture-alliance/dpa/Peter Kneffel, 34, Russ Bishop Stock Connection Worldwide, 33, ZUMA Press/TCS/Menno Boermans, 18; Science Source: BSIP, 27; Shutterstock: Andrew Arseev, 28, bikeriderlondon, 43 (bottom), Brandelet, 30, Ipatov, 9, Jim Parkin, 16, PHOTOunterwegs, 31, Rechitan Sorin, 20, Richard Thornton, 15, Robert Crum, 4

Design Elements: Shutterstock

About the Cover
A rescue team trains for the challenging recovery of a wounded hiker on the side of a mountain.

Printed in the United States of America in North Mankato, Minnesota.
032013 007223CGF13

TABLE OF CONTENTS

Mount Hood is a dormant, or inactive, volcano. The last time it was known to erupt was in 1866.

CHAPTER 1

What Do Rescue Teams Do?

Can you imagine spending the holidays away from your family, cold and **stranded** on a mountain? Mark Kelsey, Margarita Estrada, and Deborah Shindler couldn't. Lucky for them, they received a Christmas miracle. They were rescued after spending two cold and snowy nights stranded on Mount Hood in northern Oregon.

Lost in the Wilderness

On December 22, 2012, the three experienced climbers set off on a 4.7-mile (7.6-kilometer) hike. They were hoping to reach a cabin where they planned to celebrate Estrada's birthday.

But more than 6 feet (1.8 meters) of snow had fallen in the previous week, so the hikers had trouble finding and staying on the trail. When they were unable to find the cabin, they kept searching. They searched for 20 straight hours!

stranded · left behind

In the morning, they called 911 for help, but their cell phone signal was weak. Authorities were unable to track their location using the phone's **GPS (Global Positioning System)**. At that point, the Crag Rats—a group of experienced mountain rescuers—was sent to look for them.

The hikers called 911 again later in the day. This time, they were able to give their exact location, but the Crag Rats were unable to find them before nightfall.

Rescued!

On Christmas Eve, the Portland Mountain Rescue joined the search. Around 10:15 a.m., the lost hikers were found. They were tired, cold, and hungry, but they were not injured. The rescuers gave them warm drinks and snacks, but their journey was not over. They still had to climb more than 1 mile (1.6 km) uphill in deep snow and difficult **terrain** to reach a rescue vehicle. The trek took about three hours. The hikers were reunited with their families a short time later.

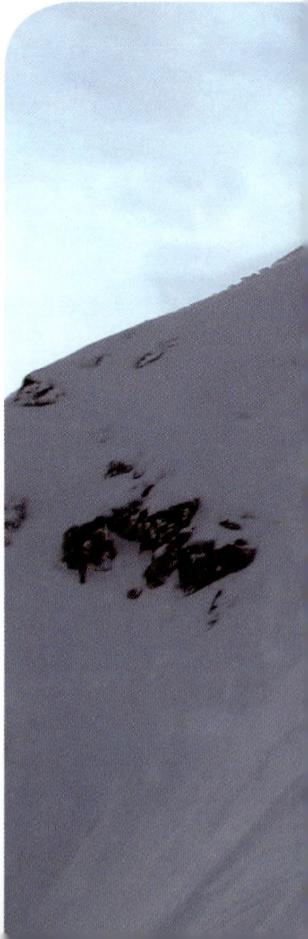

A member of the Crag Rats search and rescue team scales Mount Hood while looking for three missing hikers.

Kelsey, Estrada, and Shindler were lucky. They were all very experienced **mountaineers**. In fact, Kelsey had worked for the Portland Mountain Rescue for 18 years. They were also planning to stay overnight in the cabin, so they had brought along sleeping bags and food. It was also fortunate that their cell phone's battery didn't die. Because they were able to call 911, the rescuers were able to track them using the phone's GPS.

GPS (Global Positioning System) • an electronic tool used to find the location of an object

terrain • the surface of the land

mountaineer • a mountain climber

Who Do Mountain Rescue Teams Help?

These days, more and more people take part in activities in the mountains, such as climbing, hiking, cycling, skiing, and snowboarding. Whether they've made poor decisions or had some bad luck, many people need help from a mountain rescue team. Even professional mountain climbers can get caught in bad weather or stuck because their equipment fails.

Ready for Action

Mountain rescue teams are always ready to help people who have run into trouble. At any given time, they could be sent on a **mission** to save someone's life. Most rescuers are **volunteers**. Even so, when a call comes in that there's an emergency, these volunteers leave their regular jobs and rush to the scene.

mission • a planned job or task

volunteer • a person who chooses to do work without pay

A Grim Ending

Not every rescue story has a happy ending. In December 2006, three climbers died on Mount Hood when they got caught in an unexpected storm. Temperatures dropped to minus 40 degrees Fahrenheit (minus 40 degrees Celsius) and winds gusted at 130 miles (209 km) per hour. In an attempt to seek shelter, the men dug a snow cave. One man froze to death in the cave. At some point before the storm hit, he left his sleeping bag and heavy coat behind to lighten his load. The two other men were never found. It is believed they died when they left their injured friend to get help.

Mountain sports, such as snowboarding, are becoming more popular.

Some rescuers work at ski resorts. Ski patrol workers are often the first to respond when **avalanches** and other emergencies occur at ski resorts.

Other rescue teams work in the vast, barren area known as the **backcountry**. These areas are unmarked and unpatrolled, which makes them more dangerous.

Rescuers in Croatia practice a daring mountain rescue.

Dangers of the Job

Mountains can be very dangerous places. Rescue workers must know how to **navigate** safely from place to place in dangerous terrain. They often have to climb up and down steep cliffs to reach injured people. The cliffs may be icy and snow covered. It's very cold in the mountains and often quite windy, with heavy rain or snow.

Rescuers may also face falling rocks or ice, sudden storms, lightning, or avalanches. They must be prepared for anything.

Rocky Mountain Rescue

The Rocky Mountain Rescue Group is based in Boulder, Colorado. In 2012, the group logged 6,000 volunteer hours while responding to rescue missions and incidents. They received 163 calls for help and saved the lives of 205 people. They even rescued a rock climber who became pinned between a tree and a 1-ton (0.9-metric ton) boulder.

avalanche · a large mass of ice, snow, or earth that suddenly moves down the side of a mountain

backcountry · an area that is not marked by trails or patrolled by park rangers or other authorities

navigate · to get around or get through

Weathering the Challenge

Brave mountain rescue teams work during avalanches, floods, mudslides, blizzards, and many other **natural disasters**. The rescue team might need to go to the top of a mountain or into a raging river to save someone.

Mountain rescue workers must be prepared for any situation. High in the mountains, the weather can change very quickly. The temperature can drop, and winds can pick up. Clouds can develop, and it can start to rain or snow without much warning.

Many times, when people are lost or injured on a mountain, they call for help with a cell phone or radio. But sometimes, they are not able to get a strong enough cell phone signal to reach help. That's why it's important to always let someone know where you're going and when you'll be back. If you're not back when you say you will be, they can call for help for you.

Once a call for help comes in, the rescue team makes a plan. Then team members get their equipment and head for the mountains.

natural disaster • an earthquake, flood, storm, or other deadly event caused by nature

Rescue Fact!

During a blizzard in the mountains, winds can blow more than 100 miles (161 km) per hour.

Members of the Portland Mountain Rescue prepare for a mission on Mount Hood.

How Teams Prepare

All members of a mountain rescue team are expert mountaineers. But they still need to train for rescue missions. Regular classroom and field training is necessary for rescue teams to be well prepared for any situation.

Mountain rescue workers need to know how to use their equipment. They must learn to work closely and safely together. Well-trained rescue workers can avoid accidents.

Some rescuers are also experts in first aid. First aid is help given to an injured or sick person before they are taken to the hospital.

Rescue Fact!

The highest mountain in the world is Mount Everest, which is located in the Himalayas. These mountains are located between the countries of Nepal and Tibet. The mountain's **summit**, or top, is 29,035 feet (8,850 meters) above **sea level.**

summit • the very top of a mountain

sea level • the level of the ocean; it is used as a starting point for measuring the height of land

Knowing the Land

Rescue workers also have to study the local landscape, or surroundings, because many rescue missions involve searches. By knowing the area, rescue workers can find a victim more easily. They will know the most likely places to search first.

Rescue workers receive training on helicopter rescues.

Rescue vehicles, such as this one used by the Rocky Mountain Search and Rescue team, carry a lot of equipment.

CHAPTER 2

Getting Around

A vehicle can be a mountain rescue team's most important tool. Rescue vehicles carry workers and necessary equipment to a rescue scene.

Which Trucks Are Used?

Rescue trucks can range in size from small to huge. Many rescue teams use a pickup truck with a cover on the back to hold their supplies. Others use **command centers** that are as large as a bus.

Rescue teams need to carry a variety of tools in their trucks. These tools include ropes, anchors, **harnesses**, ladders, and other rescue equipment. The trucks also store **wet suits**, warming blankets, snacks, hot drinks, and first-aid equipment.

Rescuers also take walkie-talkies or two-way radios with them. These help them stay in touch with each other and the command center.

command center · a rescue team's home base or headquarters

harness · a device that straps one thing to another

wet suit · a close-fitting suit made of material that keeps divers warm in cold water

In the Air

Sometimes heavy snow can prevent a truck from getting to people who need help. When this happens, rescue workers use helicopters to reach areas on the mountain where trucks cannot travel.

This mountain rescue team in Switzerland receives more than 1,000 calls per year.

How Do Helicopters Help in Rescues?

Rescue helicopters carry long ropes and ladders. If the pilot cannot find a safe place to land, workers can skillfully lower ladders down to an awaiting victim. Or rescue workers can be lowered to the ground using a **winch**. If the victim is too injured to climb a ladder, helicopter crew members can lower a **stretcher** to the ground. Workers at the scene of a disaster quickly and carefully place victims on the stretcher. Then they signal for the crew on the helicopter to pull them up. Helicopters then take victims to a rescue center or a nearby hospital.

Rescue Fact!

A rescue helicopter can cost more than $10 million.

winch • a device that winds in or lets out wire; winches can be used to lift people in and out of a helicopter

stretcher • a bed with straps and wheels that medical teams use to move patients

Rescue Helicopter

Helicopters are useful when mountain roads are covered with snow and trucks can't get through. Helicopters can travel to places where trucks cannot go, such as the top or side of a mountain. Helicopters can make **vertical** landings and take off from the same **remote** location.

vertical • straight up and down

remote • far away, isolated, or distant

The pilot must hold the helicopter steady while lifting people off the ground.

Vertical mountain rescues can take four to 10 rescuers to complete.

Rescue Fact!

Members of the San Diego Mountain Rescue Team go through about 20 hours of training each month.

ledge • a narrow strip of rock that sticks out from a mountain

CHAPTER 3

Skills and Equipment

Mountain rescue workers must consider the risks involved when they are on a mission. They need to pay attention to details. They need to find solutions to problems and consider how their actions could affect others.

Physical Skills

When trucks or helicopters cannot reach an area, mountain rescue workers must use their climbing skills. If a climber is stranded on a remote mountain **ledge**, only other climbers can reach him.

Some mountain rescue missions can take days to complete. Rescuers must be in top physical shape so they can make an exhausting climb to reach the victim. After they find the victim, they must then carry out the challenging rescue. They also need to be strong enough to lift a victim to safety.

Hanging On

To climb at high elevations, or higher ground, climbers need light equipment so they don't get weighed down and tired. A sturdy rope is a mountain climber's most important piece of equipment. Most climbing ropes are made of stretchy **nylon** material and are between 0.3 and 0.4 inches (7.6 and 10 millimeters) thick.

A harness secures the climber to the rope, which is fastened to an anchor. The anchor is attached to the mountain or a heavy rock. If a climber starts to fall, the anchor will stop the climber from falling any farther than the length of the rope. Climbers should always wear a helmet.

Mountain climbers use **crampons** and ice axes to help support them as they climb mountains. Crampons are metal spikes that attach to the bottom of a climber's boots. They have up to 16 spikes on each boot. These spikes help climbers gain more secure footing on snow and ice.

The spikes on crampons are about 1 inch (2.5 centimeters) long.

nylon • an artificial fiber that makes a very strong cloth

crampon • a metal frame with pointed metal teeth that attaches to a climber's boot

Mountaintop E.R.

Mountain rescue workers always carry bandages and other first-aid supplies to rescue scenes. Many are also trained as **paramedics**. They can provide lifesaving treatment at the scene.

Rescue workers use a special kind of stretcher called an immobilizer. An immobilizer keeps a victim's back and neck from moving. An immobilizer is used when they think a victim may have a neck or spinal injury.

Rescue teams also help people suffering from "mountain sickness" or from **hypothermia**. Mountain sickness comes from a lack of **oxygen** in the body. People can die from hypothermia in as little as two hours. Rescue workers carry special warming blankets and oxygen supplies. They can help stop these dangerous conditions from getting any worse.

paramedic · a person who treats patients before they reach the hospital and also can drive an ambulance

hypothermia · a life-threatening condition that occurs when a person's body temperature falls several degrees below normal

oxygen · a colorless gas in the air that people and animals need to breathe

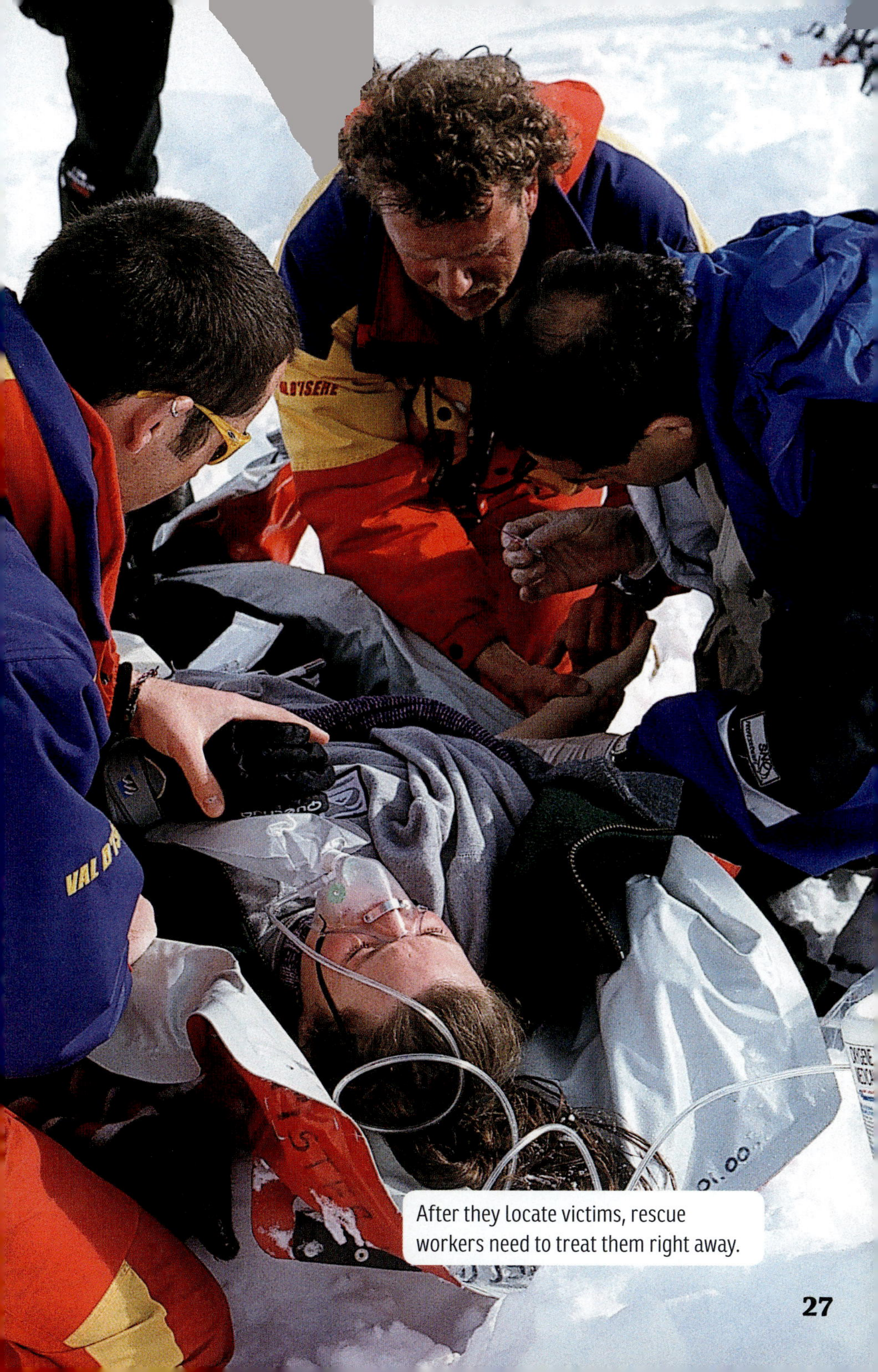

After they locate victims, rescue workers need to treat them right away.

Avalanches such as this one are unstoppable. They bury anything in their path in heavy snow, including skiers.

CHAPTER 4

Deep Snow Rescue

An avalanche is an enormous amount of snow that plummets rapidly down a mountain. Avalanches occur when loose snow starts to slide down the mountain. This can happen naturally, but people skiing, snowboarding, and snowmobiling can also cause them. Most avalanches travel at 60 to 80 miles (97 to 129 km) per hour, but some can thunder downhill at 200 miles (322 km) per hour!

Buried

Avalanches can be disastrous. They sweep away anything in their path. Avalanches can cover entire camps and bury small towns. People can get buried alive in the snow from an avalanche. From 2011 to 2012, avalanches killed 34 people in the United States.

Avalanche-related disasters require the help of mountain rescue teams. However, avalanches can occur while a rescue team is on a mission, which makes their job even more dangerous.

Keeping Track of Skiers

Rescue workers **monitor** areas where they think avalanches might occur. They watch mountain slopes for buildup of snow and ice. New technology helps them better predict when and where an avalanche might occur.

Skiers and snowboarders are at risk of being caught in avalanches. Those who travel into the backcountry are at even greater risk. Most avalanche deaths occur in the backcountry because more people are exploring these unpatrolled areas. Rescue workers try to keep track of how many people are in remote mountain areas. That way they know where to look for victims if an avalanche occurs.

People are warned to avoid areas where an avalanche is likely to occur.

GPS devices help hikers avoid getting lost and figure out their location if needed.

Technology and Avalanche Survival

Technology has made searching for missing hikers and skiers easier. Hikers often take cell phones and GPS devices with them. These help hikers determine their location. If they are lost or injured and can call for help, they can tell rescuers where to look for them.

monitor • to watch closely

Similarly, **personal locator beacons (PLBs)**, or avalanche beacons, can be attached or built into skis, snowboards, and other equipment. These devices give off a signal. When someone wearing a PLB is buried in snow, other people with beacons can pick up the signal from the buried person. In this way, the beacon guides rescuers toward the signal and to the victim.

Wearing an avalanche beacon can mean the difference between life and death. PLBs can reduce the amount of time victims are buried. But people should not take unnecessary risks just because they are wearing one. Dangerous avalanche conditions should always be avoided.

Rescue workers and skiers dig for survivors following an avalanche in Austria.

Rescue Fact!

Sixty-five percent of the people living in Switzerland live in areas where avalanches are a risk. The country builds walls around some cities. It also protects its forests, which act as natural walls against avalanches.

A rescuer uses a beacon and a probe to search for skiers buried in an avalanche.

Searching for Survivors

When an avalanche occurs, rescue teams race to the scene. They use **probes**, which are long poles that they poke into the snow to feel for bodies. Once they locate a victim, they use shovels to dig the person out of the snow.

personal locator beacon (PLB) • a tracking device that helps rescuers find lost or injured people

probe • a long pole that is used to poke under the surface of snow

How Can Dogs Help?

Dogs also play key roles on mountain rescue teams. Because of their heightened sense of smell, dogs are the best at finding people buried in snow. A well-trained dog team can search 2.5 acres (1 hectare) of land in about 30 minutes. It would take 20 rescue workers several hours to cover the same area.

Rescue workers in the German Alps try to find avalanche victims using probes and rescue dogs.

Rescue Dog Training

One of the best rescue dog training schools in the United States is the Wasatch Backcountry Rescue (WBR) International Dog School in Utah. The school offers monthly training sessions in subject areas such as wilderness search, night search, and getting comfortable riding in a helicopter. The training makes sure that dogs and rescuers work well together.

WBR dogs start training as puppies. By the time they are 1 year old, they are able to work in the ski area. By 18 months of age, they are fully trained to work on rescues in ski resorts and the backcountry. Rescue dogs usually retire when they are about 10 years old.

A rescue dog and its handler prepare for helicopter training.

Rescue Fact!

Scientists believe that a dog's sense of smell is 10,000 to 100,000 times stronger than a human's!

An Avalanche Survivor's Story

In December 2012, Emily Anderson and some friends were skiing at Crystal Mountain Ski Resort near Seattle, Washington. They had no idea what was in store for them that day.

Buried Alive

Anderson had just finished an amazing run skiing down the slopes. Suddenly, she heard a cracking sound and felt the snow move beneath her. She knew right away it was an avalanche.

As the snow thundered down the mountain, it knocked Anderson down and tossed her up against a tree. She came to a stop buried under a few feet of snow. Her right arm was stuck, but she was able to move her left hand. Anderson scooped the snow away from her mouth so she could breathe. She also screamed for help, but because she was buried in the snow, no one could hear her.

On average, Crystal Mountain gets over 40 feet (12.2 m) of snow each year.

Help Is on the Way

While Anderson was trapped, one of her friends was able to call for help. Rescuers from the ski patrol arrived quickly. They poked their probes into the snow to try to locate Anderson.

Emily Anderson was very lucky. After being buried alive under a blanket of snow for nearly 15 minutes, she felt a rescuer's probe poking her. They dug her out of the snow, and she walked away from the frightening experience with only minor injuries.

Crystal Mountain is the largest ski resort in the state of Washington with 57 ski trails.

After surviving an avalanche, Anderson didn't give up skiing. But she did decide to buy an avalanche beacon and take some avalanche safety classes. She may also become a member of the ski patrol so she can help rescue other avalanche victims.

Rescue Fact!

A completely buried avalanche victim can die within 25 minutes.

A mountain rescue worker prepares for his next mission.

CHAPTER 5

Mission Accomplished

Rescue workers put in long hours doing this important job. A rescue team's greatest reward is when a mission is successfully completed.

Volunteer Heroes

Anyone who wants to be a member of a mountain rescue team must be an expert mountaineer. Rescuers have to be very physically fit. They must also know how to find their way in the mountains at night and in bad weather. Rescue workers must be able to make quick decisions because lives depend on it.

In most mountain communities, rescue workers volunteer their time. They do not get paid for their rescue work. They volunteer to work on the rescue team because they want to help save other people. Rescue workers must always be prepared for their next mission.

Staying Safe in the Mountains

Hopefully you'll never get into trouble on a mountain and need the help of a mountain rescue team. Always follow this simple advice before you set off:

- Never go alone.
- Always tell somebody where you are going and what time you plan to be back.
- Never go if bad weather may occur.
- Dress in layers and always take warm clothes. Clothes made of wool or non-natural materials are best. Cotton is difficult to dry. Be sure to wear a windproof and a waterproof layer.
- Wear sturdy shoes with good ankle support, a firm sole, and a secure grip.
- Wear a hat, sunglasses, and sunscreen.
- Take along high-energy snacks, such as bagels, fruit, granola bars, peanut butter, and trail mix.
- Make sure you bring along enough water or sports drinks. Take about 2 quarts (1.9 liters) of water per person per day. Avoid drinking soda when you're hiking. Don't drink from streams. You could get sick if you don't clean the water.
- Carry a first-aid kit, flashlight, whistle, solar blanket, and matches to start a fire.
- Take a fully charged cell phone and an extra battery if you have it. Also bring a compass, a map of the area, and a GPS device (with extra battery power).
- In an emergency, don't be afraid to call for help. Most places do not charge for search and rescue services.

If you go hiking in the mountains, be sure to take along snacks, water, and safety gear.

Knowing how to use a compass and read a trail map are basic skills that every hiker should know.

Read More

Camerena, Rebecca. *My Dog Is a Hero.* New York: Scholastic, 2012.

Garbe, Suzanne. *The Worst Avalanches of All Time.* Epic Disasters. North Mankato, Minn.: Capstone Press, 2013.

Green, Sara. *Snow Search Dogs.* Dogs to the Rescue! Minneapolis: Bellwether Media, Inc., 2014.

Oxlade, Chris. *Mountain Rescue.* Heroic Jobs. Chicago: Raintree, 2012.

Pipe, Jim. *Rescue Squad: Saving Lives.* Mission Impossible. Redding, Conn.: Brown Bear Books, 2011.

Internet Sites

FactHound offers a safe, fun way to find Internet sites related to this book. All of the sites on FactHound have been researched by our staff.

Here's all you do:
Visit *www.facthound.com*
Type in this code: 9781625210623

Glossary of Text Features

Text Feature	How to Use It
Caption: A word or group of words shown with a picture or illustration	Read a caption to understand information that may not be in the text.
Diagram: A drawing that shows or explains something	Examine a diagram to understand steps in a process, how something is made, or the parts of something.
Glossary: List of key terms with their meanings	Look up key terms in the glossary to find their meanings and to get a better understanding of the topic of the text.
Index: Alphabetical list of key terms, names, and topics in a text with their page numbers	Use the index to find pages that contain information you are looking for.
Map: A drawing that represents a place, such as a country or city	Use a map to understand relative locations and determine where events took place.
Photograph or Illustration: Visuals that are created by cameras or drawn	Examine photographs and illustrations to better understand ideas in the text that might be unclear.
Subhead: Word or group of words that divides the text into sections and tells the main idea of a section	Use subheads to locate information in the text and understand how a text is organized.
Table: Represents data in a small space	Examine a table to understand data or to compare information in the text.
Table of Contents: List of the major parts of the book and their page numbers	Use a table of contents to locate general information in the text and see how the topics are organized.
Text Box: A box in the text that provides extra information about a topic	Read a text box to understand interesting or important information.
Text Style: Bold, color, or italic words in the text	Pay attention to bold, italic, and color words to figure out which words in the text are important.
Timeline: Shows events in the order in which they occurred	Use a timeline to understand the order in which events occurred or how one event led to another.

Glossary

avalanche (A-vuh-lanch) • a large mass of ice, snow, or earth that suddenly moves down the side of a mountain

backcountry (BAK kuhn-tree) • an area that is not marked by trails or patrolled by park rangers or other authorities

command center (kuh-MAND SEN-tur) • a rescue team's home base or headquarters

crampon (KRAM-pahn) • a metal frame with pointed metal teeth that attaches to a climber's boot

GPS (Global Positioning System) (GLOH-buhl puh-ZI-shuh-ning SISS-tuhm) • an electronic tool used to find the location of an object

harness (HAR-niss) • a device that straps one thing to another

hypothermia (hye-puh-THUR-mee-uh) • a life-threatening condition that occurs when a person's body temperature falls several degrees below normal

ledge (LEJ) • a narrow strip of rock that sticks out from a mountain

mission (MISH-uhn) • a planned job or task

monitor (MON-uh-tur) • to watch closely

mountaineer (moun-tuh-NIHR) • a mountain climber

natural disaster (NACH-ur-uhl di-ZAS-tuhr) • an earthquake, flood, storm, or other deadly event caused by nature

navigate (NAV-uh-gate) • to get around or get through

nylon (NYE-lon) • an artificial fiber that makes a very strong cloth

oxygen (OK-suh-juhn) • a colorless gas in the air that people and animals need to breathe

paramedic (pa-ruh-MEH-dik) • a person who treats patients before they reach the hospital and also can drive an ambulance

personal locator beacon (PLB) (PUR-suh-nuhl LOH-kate-or BEE-kuhn) • a tracking device that helps rescuers find lost or injured people

probe (PROHB) • a long pole that is used to poke under the surface of snow

remote (ri-MOHT) • far away, isolated, or distant

sea level (SEE LEV-uhl) • the level of the ocean; it is used as a starting point for measuring the height of land

stranded (STRAN-did) • left behind

stretcher (STRECH-ur) • a bed with straps and wheels that medical teams use to move patients

summit (SUHM-it) • the very top of a mountain

terrain (tuh-RAYN) • the surface of the land

vertical (VUR-tuh-kuhl) • straight up and down

volunteer (vol-uhn-TIHR) • a person who chooses to do work without pay

wet suit (WET SOOT) • a close-fitting suit made of material that keeps divers warm in cold water

winch (WINCH) • a device that winds in or lets out wire; winches can be used to lift people in and out of a helicopter

Index